The Lunch Lady's Daughter

by Roderick J. Robison

Also by Roderick J. Robison
The Lunch Lady's Daughter 2
Middle School Millionaires
The Principal's Son
The Magic Water
The Christmas Tin

For Ana Clara

Table of Contents

Chapter 1
June 20, 2002

Sarah McKinliy glanced up at the clock. Two minutes until the final bell—and the start of summer vacation. Sarah sighed. Unlike the other students in her class, Sarah did *not* want the school year to end. Not at all. She liked fourth grade just fine, thank you very much.

She was very shy. Sarah had always been quiet. She rarely raised her hand in class to volunteer answers. And she hardly ever participated in classroom discussions. On her midterm progress reports, her teachers wrote comments like *needs to participate more in classroom discussion, seems reserved, should be more assertive,* and *rarely asks questions in class.*

Sarah always did her best to blend into the crowd, never did anything to draw attention to herself. Attention was the last thing she wanted. But fifth grade would not be like her other years at J.T. Tideville Elementary School. Not at all.

She absolutely dreaded the thought of starting fifth grade in September, wished she could repeat fourth grade. Other kids might be able to handle the transition to fifth grade if they were in her shoes. But other kids were not in *her* shoes. Their mother would not be their fifth grade teacher.

Sarah would be the *teacher's daughter*. And she absolutely dreaded the attention that would result from being the teacher's kid. She would no longer be able to just blend into the crowd. Sarah was already bracing herself for the teasing and taunts that would surely result from being the teacher's daughter.

She had known for some time that her mother would be her fifth grade teacher. Her mother started teaching at the school when Sarah was a second-grader. Back then, fifth-grade seemed light years away.

Brriiiiinngg!

Sarah winced. Summer vacation had officially begun.

"Have a great summer, ya'll," Mrs. Timsen said to the class. "Thanks for all of the hard work this year."

Fifth grade was already drawing closer. Sarah's hands got clammy just thinking about it.

Chapter 2

When she got home that afternoon, Sarah was surprised to see her mother sitting at the kitchen table. Her mother was reading a novel. Usually at this time of the day, the woman was busy preparing dinner. Her mother loved to cook.

Her mother looked up when Sarah stepped into the kitchen. "Hi, sweetheart."

"Hey, Mom…what are you doing?"

"I'm reading a novel."

"Uh huh…but what about dinner?"

Mrs. McKinliy smiled. "Your father is bringing dinner home tonight. He said we're going to celebrate. He has some news he is going to share with us."

"News?"

"That's right."

"What kind of news?"

Sarah's mother shrugged. "I don't know. Your father didn't give any hints. It sounds like he wants to surprise us."

"Huh."

Mr. McKinliy pulled into the driveway at seven o'clock that evening. Sarah was upstairs in her room. She looked out the window and saw her dad remove a large paper bag of take-out food from the front seat of the car. Sarah recognized the logo on the bag. The food was from the Mexican restaurant downtown. Sarah loved Mexican food!

Mr. McKinliy didn't disclose the news right away when he stepped into the house. He waited until Sarah and her mom were seated at the dinner table. And then he made an announcement. "Good news!" he boomed. "I received a promotion at work today."

Sarah's mom's eye brows rose. "Congratulations, sweetheart!"

"That's great, Dad," Sarah put in.

Mr. McKinliy looked at his wife and daughter. "There's more...I'm being transferred."

"Transferred?"

"Yes, I'm being transferred...up north."

"Up *north*?"

"That's right. My new position is in Massachusetts. The company opened a new site up there a few months ago."

Sarah's mother's eyebrows lifted. "Wow...this certainly is big news, sweetheart. And a surprise."

Sarah smiled. She was relieved—her mother would not be her teacher in the fall.

"This move will be a good thing for us," Mr. McKinliy said.

"I guess I should start looking for a job," Sarah's mother announced. Sarah hoped her mother would find a job in Massachusetts—as long as it didn't involve teaching fifth grade at her new school.

"When do we move, Dad?"

"Next month."

"Cool."

* * * * *

The new neighborhood in Massachusetts was nice enough. But it was unusually quiet. There were no kids around when the McKinliys moved into their new home. Sarah ventured around town the day after moving in. She went to the town pool, a park, a playground, and a small strip mall. And she visited the library too. But there were no kids her age at any of those places either. It seemed strange.

It wasn't until her third day in the new neighborhood that Sarah saw someone her age. It was just after she woke up that morning. Sarah's bedroom window faced the sidewalk. She looked out her bedroom window and saw a girl walking down the sidewalk. Sarah only caught a glimpse of the girl as she walked by. By the time she got up and made her way to the window…the girl was gone.

Sarah stumbled into the kitchen for a bowl of cereal. Her dad was eating breakfast at the kitchen table.

"Morning, kiddo."

"Morning, Dad." Sarah sighed.

"Why the sad face?"

"I'm bored."

Her father smiled. "Don't worry. You'll make some new friends soon."

Sarah hoped so. She was shy, but she was not antisocial. She did want to meet other kids and make some new friends. But things were not looking good so far. "It seems like there aren't many kids around here."

"They're probably just away at summer camp or on vacation," her father remarked.

"Maybe you're right, Dad."

A week passed. The neighborhood was still as quiet as ever. Sarah spent most of her days at the library. And she visited the dime store often too. She had discovered the store during her first trip downtown. It was a place she never grew tired of.

When Sarah woke up on the first morning of August, she looked out her bedroom window and saw the girl again, walking down the sidewalk. She was about Sarah's height, and had long black hair pulled back into a pony tail. Sarah got up and walked toward the window. But by the time she opened the window...the girl was gone. Again.

That afternoon, after spending a few hours at the library, Sarah stopped by the dime store. When she made her way over to the cosmetics section, another girl was there. A girl with long black hair. The girl she had seen on the sidewalk that morning. She was holding a tube of lipstick.

The girl didn't see Sarah; her back was toward Sarah. Sarah made her way down the aisle and slowly approached the girl. She said, "Hi."

8

The girl jumped in surprise and slowly turned around and looked at Sarah.

"*Hola—Hi*," the girl replied. She quickly placed the lipstick on a shelf and walked out of the store. It seemed the girl was just as shy as Sarah.

Sarah followed the girl out of the store. She caught up with her on the sidewalk. "Wait." Sarah said.

The girl stopped and turned around.

Are you...*Spanish*?" Sarah asked.

A look of surprise crossed the girl's face. And then she smiled. "*Si—Yes*." But how did you know?"

"You said *hola*."

"Do you speak *Spanish*?" the girl inquired.

Sarah shook her head. "No."

The girl's eyebrows lifted. She seemed confused. "I don't understand. You do not speak Spanish, but you knew when I said *hi* in Spanish?"

Sarah smiled. "There was a Mexican restaurant where I used to live. We ate there a lot. I picked up a few words."

"Oh...you like Mexican food?"

Sarah nodded. "Yes. Very much."

The girl smiled.

9

The girl's name was Mariana. They only lived two blocks away from each other.

And the two of them quickly became friends.

They spent every day in August together. They usually started their day down at the town pool, except for Tuesdays. Tuesday was movie day at the library.

Sometimes they took the bus to the mall. And they did some sleepovers too. Mariana spent a few nights at Sarah's house. Under Sarah's mother's supervision, they baked apple pies for dessert.

And Sarah stayed overnight at Mariana's house a few times. Mariana's mother taught them how to make *bonbons*—chocolate-filled sweets.

One day, Sarah said to Mariana, "I haven't seen anyone else our age around here since moving in. Where are your friends?"

Mariana did not answer at first. A sad look crossed her face. Then she said, "I do not have any other friends. You are my *only* friend."

"You don't have *any* other friends?" Sarah found this hard to believe. Mariana was a great person. And she was pretty, too. *How can she not have friends?*

"That's right," Mariana admitted. "When we moved here last year, I did not speak English so well. And none of the kids at school spoke Spanish."

"You speak English very well, now," Sarah observed.

"Si—Yes. But it was not always so."

"*Nobody* tried to make friends with you?" Sarah asked.

Mariana shook her head. "No. But now there is you."

"We'll always be friends," Sarah said.

*****

On the last Friday of summer vacation, they were lying down on towels along the edge of the town pool. Sarah's transistor radio was tuned to their favorite station. There were actually some other kids around now. It seemed kids had returned from camp over the past few days.

Sarah and Mariana hadn't been there long when a group of three girls passed by them on their way to the snack bar. They appeared to be their age. The tallest of the three, an attractive girl with deep brown eyes and long blond hair, was doing most of the talking; Sarah guessed she was the leader...And she was surprised when the girl

11

narrowed her eyes at Mariana as the three of them walked by.

Sarah wasn't sure if Mariana had picked up on it.

"Do you know them?" Sarah asked.

Mariana nodded. "Yes. They are in our grade at school."

Chapter 3
Thursday, September 5th

The first day of school. A large group of students and parents were gathered in front of the entrance to H.C. Stonewelle Elementary School. The students' bright new first-day-of-school clothes contrasted sharply against the dark bricks of the school building.

When the first bell rang, the crowd funneled slowly into the school. Inside the building, the hallways were loud as students shouted to friends they hadn't seen since June. The second bell was barely audible over the din of voices and slamming lockers.

Sarah found her locker outside Room 210—her new classroom. Mariana's locker was further down the hall by her classroom, Room 215.

"I wish we were in the same class," Sarah told Mariana as she opened her locker.

"Me too," Mariana quietly replied.

"Well, we'll probably have the same lunch period," Sarah said hopefully. "We can eat together."

13

Mariana nodded. "That would be good," she said. "See you later."

Sarah entered Room 210 just at the start of the morning announcements. Most of her classmates were already seated. The desks were arranged in five orderly rows.

The teacher, Ms. Zebulane, was hovering by the door when Sarah stepped into the classroom. The woman was dressed in clothing from an earlier time: flared jeans and a vibrant embroidered blouse. Hooped earrings dangled from the woman's ear lobes and draped around her neck was a thick beaded necklace.

"Good morning," Ms. Zebulane said, glancing down at her seating chart. "You must be Sarah."

Sarah nodded. "Yes."

Ms. Zebulane smiled. "Welcome. Third row, fourth seat."

"Thanks."

Sarah glanced around the room. There were peace signs and smiley faces on the walls. A beaded curtain delineated the reading area at the back of the room. The 1960's theme was interesting. It was a much different than the theme in her fourth grade classroom at her old school.

Sarah didn't know any of the students. But she did recognize one person. The girl sitting in the fourth seat of the fourth row—right beside Sarah's assigned seat. The tall, blonde girl from the pool. She smiled at Sarah as she sat down.

Ms. Zebulane took attendance. Then she said, "We're going to be seeing a lot of each other this year. You'll be in this room for most of your core subjects—everything except for music, art and PE. But, before we dive into formalities and get underway, we'll have a little get-acquainted session. I'd like to learn a little bit about you and hear about your summer. But I don't want *you* to tell me these things. You will interview the person sitting beside you. You'll ask that person about their favorite sport or hobby. And find out what they did over the summer. Then you'll share the information with the class."

"Those in the first row will interview the person beside you in the second row, and the same for the third and fourth rows. You may begin. You have five minutes."

Sarah glanced over at the girl from the pool. The girl moved her seat so it faced Sarah's. "I'm Bonnie," the girl said.

"Sarah."

15

"Where are you from?" Bonnie asked.

"Virginia. We just moved up here over the summer."

"What did you *do* over the summer?" Bonnie inquired.

Sarah told Bonnie that she spent most of the summer at the town pool and at the library. Bonnie nodded. Then she asked, "And your favorite sport is…?"

Sarah thought for a moment. "I like to skate."

Bonnie smiled. "I like to skate too! Now it's your turn to ask me questions."

"Okay," Sarah said. "Tell me about your summer."

Bonnie rambled on about the overnight camp she and her two friends had attended. She talked about pillow fights, horseback riding, and competitions against kids at the neighboring camp. Bonnie reported that the pool at camp was much better than the town pool.

After each student told the class about what they had learned from the classmate they interviewed, Ms. Zebulane distributed the class schedule, journals, textbooks and workbooks. Reality was quickly setting in. Summer vacation was officially over.

"As you'll see on the class schedule," Ms. Zebulane announced, "we're starting with math."

A number of students groaned. Ms. Zebulane smiled. "I know, I know. This is a big adjustment. I miss summer too. But you're here to *learn*. And I'm paid to *teach*. Open your math books. We'll start on page ten."

Ms. Zebulane droned on about fractions and decimals for hours, it seemed. Like Sarah's former teachers, the woman asked a lot questions and encouraged classroom participation. Though Sarah knew the answers, she didn't raise her hand to volunteer answers. Just like at her old school.

Brriiiiinngg!

Sarah glanced up at the clock. *Lunchtime.*

She followed the other students out of the room. Out in the hallway, Sarah did her best to blend into the crowd. She never did anything to draw attention to herself. Attention was the last thing she wanted.

*****

The lunch line in the cafeteria was much shorter than the one at her old school— which was surprising because there were more students at H.C. Stonewelle Elementary School than at her old school. A lot more.

Sarah made her way over to the lunch line. Randall Kepleire was in front of her. He was the most talkative student in Ms. Zebulane's classroom. The kid had been voted class clown back in fourth grade.

"I'll have a steak, medium rare," Randall told the lunch lady. "And potatoes au gratin with a side of steamed asparagus."

The lunch lady—an elderly woman with a kind smile—handed him a plate of lunch: a hotdog encased in soggy dough, dehydrated mashed potatoes topped with questionable gravy, and a clump of beans.

"Yum! Another delicacy," Randall said. "Can't wait to dig in." Randall placed the plate on his lunch tray and pushed the tray down the rail toward the dessert shelf. He passed on dessert—green jello topped with stale whipped cream. The whipped cream looked like it had solidified.

When Sarah reached the serving area, she too was disappointed when the lunch lady handed her a plate laden with the *daily special*. The lunch didn't compare to the meals at her old school. It wasn't even close.

Sarah passed on dessert too. Just before she reached the cash register, she grabbed a pint of lukewarm milk from an unrefrigerated case. Then she proceeded to the cash register.

"Three dollars," the attendant behind the cash register wheezed.

Sarah handed the woman three dollars and headed out into the lunchroom. The place was loud. And most of the tables were already filled. Sarah was looking for Mariana when she heard someone call her name. It was Bonnie. She was sitting at a table in the middle of the lunchroom with the two girls from the pool and several other girls.

Bonnie waved to Sarah. "Sit with us!" she shouted.

Sarah walked over to the table. There was one seat available directly across the table from Bonnie. She made her way over to the seat and placed her tray on the table. As Sarah sat down…she noticed that everyone else at the table had brought their lunch from home. She seemed to recall that Mariana had brought her lunch too.

Bonnie introduced Sarah to the other two girls from the pool: Claire and Lauren.

"Where are you from?" Claire asked.

"She is from Virginia," Bonnie answered, before Sarah could reply.

"That's right," Sarah confirmed.

"My dad was stationed in Virginia when he was in the Navy," Lauren put in.

"Norfolk?" Sarah asked.

Lauren nodded. "Yes."

"I lived in a small town a little south of Norfolk," Sarah told her.

"Sarah likes skating," Bonnie announced.

"Come to my birthday party on Saturday!" Claire said. "We're going skating at the town arena."

"Thanks. I'd like that."

"I'll bring you an invitation tomorrow."

"Great."

For a shy kid, Sarah thought she was off to a good start. But then Bonnie, Claire and Lauren started talking about the camp they had attended over the summer. And the other girls at the table joined in on the conversation too. Sarah suddenly began to feel like an outcast. She looked around for Mariana, felt guilty now for not joining her for lunch.

A few minutes later, Bonnie suddenly stopped talking. She stared across the cafeteria. Her eyes narrowed, just like the day at the pool. Sarah looked across the room to see what had captured Bonny's attention…It was Mariana. Mariana was walking across the cafeteria to discard her lunch bag.

"That girl is *weird*," Bonnie said, motioning to Mariana.

It was apparent that Bonnie didn't realize that Sarah and Mariana were friends. Sarah had been wearing sunglasses and a wide-brimmed hat that day at the pool. Bonnie must not have realized that she was the person on the towel beside Mariana that day. She obviously hadn't made the connection.

*****

Sarah caught up with Mariana on the way home from school. "Sorry about not catching up with you at lunch," she said. "I looked for you and didn't see you. Then a girl from my class invited me to sit at her table."

"It is no problem," Mariana said.

Their path took them by Sarah's house. They stopped in front of Sarah's house. Mariana said, "My parents and I are going apple-picking on Saturday. Would you like to go?"

Sarah hesitated. "I'd like to…but I got invited to a birthday party on Saturday."

Mariana grew silent. "Okay. See you tomorrow."

*****

It was just Sarah and her mother at the dinner table that night. Mr. McKinliy was working late. Sarah had a larger appetite than usual.

"My, you sure are hungry tonight," her mother commented.

"I'm starved," Sarah said.

"Didn't you have lunch at school today?"

Sarah winced. "I didn't finish lunch."

"How come?"

"It was…horrible."

Her mother's eyebrows lifted. "It couldn't have been *that* bad."

"Trust me. It was."

"Well, I'm sure the school lunch will be better tomorrow."

I hope so.

Chapter 4

Randall Kepleire was in front of Sarah in the lunch line again the following day. "Hmmm. Let's see," Randall said. "Today, I'll have the *filet mignon*." The lunch lady handed him a plate of dry meatloaf, mashed potatoes, and green beans that were anything but fresh.

"Wow." Randal said sarcastically. "This is the best lunch yet. Double yum!"

Sarah was equally disappointed with the food when the lunch lady handed her a plate of lunch. *Yuck!*

She pushed her tray down the rail. Like the previous day, she passed on dessert—the same green jello with stale whipped cream. Sarah grabbed a pint of lukewarm milk from the unrefrigerated case by the register and paid the attendant three dollars for a lunch she knew she wouldn't finish.

Sarah looked for Mariana when she stepped out into the lunchroom, but Mariana hadn't arrived yet. And then Bonnie called to her. "Over here, Sarah."

Bonnie, Claire, Lauren, and the others were sitting at the same table as the day before. Sarah walked over and joined them.

Claire handed Sarah an invitation to her birthday party. And the conversation at the table focused on the upcoming birthday party. All of the girls at the table were going. Then the conversation shifted to summer camp, just like the day before. Sarah had little to contribute to the conversation. Once again, she felt left out and wished she had sat with Mariana.

Chapter 5

Her father dropped her off at the town arena at two o'clock Saturday afternoon. Sarah had been looking forward to the birthday party. She was glad she had been invited.

When she stepped into the arena, the place was surprisingly cold. Sarah soon understood why the place was so frigid. It was not a *roller* skating arena like the one back home. It was an *ice* skating arena. Sarah had never skated on ice before. She had never even laced up a pair of ice skates.

Bonnie, Claire, Lauren and the other girls from the lunch table were seated on a bench next to the snack stand. They were lacing up their skates. Bonnie saw Sarah across the room. "Over here, Sarah!"

Sarah walked over to the group. "There's a pair of skates reserved for you," Claire said. She pointed to the skate rental counter. "Just tell the man behind the counter you're with the birthday party group."

"Okay, thanks."

When Sarah returned to the bench with her skates, the others were already out on the ice. Sarah laced up her skates…and then she slowly walked over to the ice. She cautiously stepped onto the ice…and froze. She was terrified.

Ice skating was much different than roller skating, Sarah quickly learned. It was a whole new world. She walked over to the boards at the edge of the rink. She breathed a sigh of relief when she reached them and grabbed onto the top edge of the boards for support.

So far, so good. After a few moments, Sarah began to slowly pull her self along the perimeter of the rink. After a while, she found the courage to let go of the boards.

She walked on the ice parallel to the boards at first. And then she started to slowly glide, keeping the boards within arms reach. Sarah was just starting to feel more comfortable on the ice when Bonnie called to her from the center of the rink. All of the girls from the birthday party had congregated in the center of the rink—about fifty feet away from Sarah. "Come join us," Bonnie called.

Oh no!

Moving away from the boards and leaving the relative safety of the edge of the rink was a scary thought. Crossing fifty feet of ice would be challenging. There were so many people on the ice—and all of them were skating so fast.

Sarah slowly turned toward the group of girls at the center of the rink. Then she began to make her way across the ice, holding her arms out for balance. She walked at first. Then she kicked off with her right foot and began to slowly glide across the ice.

It was slow going. All of the girls at the center of the rink were watching her. "You're doing good," Claire shouted.

"Sure, *real* good," Bonnie chuckled.

Sarah was more than half way there when a group of boys came skating up the ice toward her. They were playing tag. There were four of them. Sarah was right in their path. Two of the boys whizzed by on her left. The other two sped by on her right. One of them brushed Sarah on the way by…just enough to make her lose her balance.

Sarah panicked. Her arms flailed as she tried to regain her balance. She quickly lost control. Her feet went out from under her and then she was in the air…falling. Sarah crashed onto the ice and the next thing she knew, she was laying on her back.

"Bravo!" Bonnie shouted.

The crowd at the center off the rink erupted in laughter. It was quite a spectacle. How Sarah wished she had gone apple picking with Mariana.

Chapter 6

The mishap on the ice haunted Sarah that weekend. She had never felt so embarrassed. Sarah hoped the girls at the birthday party would forget about the incident. And when she arrived at Room 210 on Monday morning, it appeared that may be the case. Bonnie didn't mention anything about the skating accident. *Perhaps I worried for nothing*, Sarah thought.

When she arrived the lunch table that afternoon for fifth grade lunch period, Sarah saw there were no seats available at the table. Somebody had placed a backpack on the seat she usually sat at. And when Bonnie saw Sarah, she smirked and said, "Hey Sarah, are you going skating today?"

Laughter erupted at the table. It was like Saturday all over again. Obviously, the girls at the table had not forgotten about her mishap on the ice. Sarah suspected the incident would probably haunt her into middle school, maybe even high school. She looked downward and walked away.

Mariana was not in the cafeteria; she was at a dentist appointment. Sarah found an empty table across the room. She made her way over to it. She sighed as she set her tray on the table and sat down.

It was only September. And already she couldn't wait for the school year to end. Fifth grade was going to be one long year—if she could survive it.

*****

Sarah caught up with Mariana on the way home from school that afternoon. "Want to come over my house?" Sarah asked.

Mariana smiled. "Okay."

An hour later they were watching television in the living room at Sarah's house when someone knocked on the front door. Sarah got up and opened the door. A woman was standing on the front stoop. She was dressed in formal attire. And the woman was holding a clipboard.

"Hello," the woman said. "Are your parents home?"

Sarah nodded. "My mother is. Hold on." She went to the kitchen and told her mother about the woman at the front door. Mrs. McKinliy placed the tray of brownies she

31

had just removed from the oven on the countertop. Then she followed Sarah to the living room.

"Can I help you?" Mrs. McKinliy asked the woman.

"I hope so," the woman said with a smile.

Sarah stood beside her mother and listened. The woman worked for a marketing agency. Her client was opening a new restaurant downtown and had hired her marketing agency to survey the surrounding neighborhoods. It seemed the client was trying to ascertain which types of food would sell best in the neighborhood. The woman had been tasked with surveying the neighborhood.

"The survey will just take a few minutes," the woman said. "There are only ten questions."

"No problem," Mrs. McKinliy said. "Please, come inside. We can sit in the living room."

"Thank you."

Mrs. McKinliy and the woman sat down on the living room couch. Sarah and Mariana sat across from them in easy chairs.

"Okay," the woman said. "Question one. Which of the four types of food do you find most appealing: American, Italian, Chinese, or French?"

Sarah's mother thought for a moment. Then she said, "Italian."

The woman nodded and noted the answer. "Question two: Which of the following types of desert would you most likely order: cheesecake, pie, ice cream, or cake?"

Mrs. McKinliy looked at Sarah and Mariana. "How about it, girls?"

"Cheesecake," said Sarah.

Mariana nodded in agreement. "Yes, cheesecake."

The woman put a check mark next to cheesecake on the survey. Then she said, "Question three. Which of the following beverages would you most likely order with a meal: coffee, tea, water, soda, beer, or wine?"

"I'm a *coffee person*," Sarah's mom answered.

The woman wrote a check mark next to coffee. Then she went on to ask more questions. She asked questions about pricing, hours of operation, favorite appetizers, and décor.

When the woman finished with the survey, she gave Sarah's mother a coupon for a free meal. "The first meal is on the house when the new restaurant opens," she said. "Thanks for your time today."

After the woman left, Sarah said, "I wish someone would conduct a survey about the school lunch. I think they'd find that students would rather eat something different than what is served in the school cafeteria."

Mrs. McKinliy's eye brows lifted. "What's stopping you? Go for it. Sometimes surveys can be helpful. Surveys can sometimes capture attention and help turn things around."

"You mean *we* could conduct our own survey?" Mariana asked.

Mrs. McKinley nodded. "Sure, why not?"

Chapter 7

The next day at lunch, Sarah scanned the cafeteria for Mariana. She was done sitting with Bonnie and her cohorts at their lunch table. She saw Mariana sitting at a table across the lunchroom and headed in that direction. Mariana's face lit up when Sarah approached and set her tray down on the table. It was just the two of them.

Sarah looked at the lunch Mariana had brought from home. It looked delicious. "I have to start bringing my lunch," Sarah said.

Mariana looked at the food on Sarah's tray and nodded. "Yes. That would probably be best."

Though Sarah didn't care for the lunch, she ate quickly. She had found that it was best to eat quickly when you didn't care for the food. Better to just get it over with. There were still fifteen minutes left in the lunch period when Sarah finished her lunch. She reached into her backpack and pulled out a notepad. "I guess now would be as good a time as any to draft a survey about school lunch."

"Yes," Mariana agreed. "Now is good. I have some ideas for questions."

"Me too."

Sarah and Mariana began to brainstorm questions for the survey. Kids at nearby tables looked over at them curiously. One of them was Lizzy Zwickermin. Lizzy was sitting by herself at the table behind Sarah and Mariana's. She was perhaps the most talkative and least shy fifth-grader at H.C. Stonewelle Elementary School. Lizzy never hesitated to voice her opinion. She didn't care what other kids thought of her. And this didn't exactly make her the most popular student in school. Like Mariana and Sarah, she didn't have many friends.

Lizzy picked up her lunch tray and carried it over to Sarah and Mariana's table. She placed her tray down on their table and took a seat. "What are you writing?" she asked.

Sarah and Mariana exchanged glances.

"We're drafting a survey," Sarah said.

"A survey? What kind of survey?"

"It is a lunch survey," Mariana replied. "About the school lunch."

"Sounds like a good idea. But what's your goal?"

Sarah shrugged. "We're just hoping to create awareness…and maybe improve the school lunches."

36

"Cool. I'm all for that. I think everybody here would be. Can I see what you have so far?"

"Sure." Sarah handed the survey to Lizzy. Lizzy looked it over. Sarah and Mariana had only come up with two questions so far:

1. How often do you buy school lunch?

2. How would you rate school lunches on a scale of 1-10?

"Interesting," Lizzy said. "This is a good start. You might also want to ask about favorite foods. And maybe something about desserts and beverages too."

"Would you like to help us?" Sarah asked.

Lizzy flashed a smile. "You bet."

The three of them brainstormed for the rest of the lunch period. And by the end of the lunch period, they had come up with six additional questions.

"Now what?" Lizzy asked.

"Uh…we haven't gotten that far yet," Sarah said. "I suppose we type up the survey?"

"Tell you what," Lizzy said. "You type the survey up tonight and print some copies. We'll distribute the surveys tomorrow at lunch."

Sarah and Mariana glanced at each other. "*Distribute* them?"

"Sure. We'll hand them out at the beginning of lunch period tomorrow. Students can fill them out during lunch period and return them to *our* table before the end of lunch."

"How many surveys do you think we'll need?" Mariana inquired.

Lizzy thought for a moment. Then she said, "Well, there are probably around 75 fifth-graders. And just as many fourth-graders. A hundred and fifty should do."

"Okay," Sarah said.

"We should probably bring some pens to the cafeteria tomorrow too," Lizzy said. "I'll be in charge of that."

Brriiiiinngg!

Lunch period had come to end. But a new friendship had just begun.

"See you tomorrow...partners," Lizzy said.

Sarah and Mariana glanced at each other. What had they gotten themselves into?

Chapter 8

When Sarah got home that afternoon, she went up to her room and turned on her PC. Then she got down to business. She Googled "surveys" and reviewed a number of different surveys online, looking for formatting ideas. Soon, she came to the realization that surveys weren't as simple to write as she first figured.

She went through more than a half dozen drafts, tossing each one in the recycling basket beside her desk, before she finally came up with a survey that seemed acceptable. Sarah printed 150 copies of the survey. Then she went downstairs for dinner. Her part was done.

*****

When Sarah and Mariana arrived at the cafeteria for lunch the following day, Lizzy was waiting for them at the entrance. Lizzy waved to them as they approached. "Do you have the surveys?" she asked Sarah.

Sarah nodded. She reached into her backpack, extracted a stack of 150 surveys, and handed them to Lizzy.

"Great," said Lizzy. "We've got work to do. It would probably be best to hand them out right here."

Lizzy divided the stack of surveys into three piles. She handed one pile to Sarah and another to Mariana. She kept one pile for herself.

The fourth-graders were just arriving for lunch. Lizzy stopped a fourth-grader on his way to the lunch line. "Hi," she said, handing the kid a survey. "This is a lunch survey. If you could fill it out and return it to us by the end of lunch—it would be appreciated. And your answers might just help improve the school lunch."

"Cool, the boy said. I'm sick of school lunches."

"Just fill the survey out," Lizzy instructed. "And return it to one of us. We'll be at that table right over there." She motioned to their table across the room.

"I'm on it. Can I have some for the others at my table?"

Lizzy flashed a smile. "You bet. How many friends do you have at your table?"

"Seven."

Lizzy handed him seven more surveys.

"I guess that's all there is to it," Lizzy said to Sarah and Mariana.

Suddenly there was a stream of students headed down the hallway toward the cafeteria. "Here we go."

Sarah, Mariana, and Lizzy handed out surveys at a rapid pace over the next ten minutes. Some kids took just one; others took multiple surveys. There was excitement in the air as word of the survey spread through the lunchroom. Soon, the roar of lunch crowd could be heard all the way down at the front office.

Principal Bruntweil could hear the noise from his office. He wasn't able to check the noise out himself though. He had a conference call scheduled. He called the school secretary. "Margaret, could you go down to the cafeteria and find out what all the commotion is about?"

"Yes, sir. Right away."

"Thank you, Margaret," the principal said as he shut the door to his office.

A parent walked into the front office just as the school secretary was about to leave. The man was there to turn in a health form for his daughter and he had a question. Then the phone rang. And the fax buzzed with incoming correspondence.

By the time the school secretary reached the cafeteria, the noise was gone; the crowd had dispersed and lunch period was over. The music teacher, Ms. Bastille, had lunch duty that day. The school secretary approached her. "What was all the commotion about?" she asked.

The music teacher walked over to a table and picked up a survey. She handed the survey to the school secretary. "This is what the commotion was about."

The school secretary read the survey. "*Who* is behind the survey?" she inquired.

"Three girls—fifth-graders."

"Do you know their names?"

"Yes, I know who they are. I'll write their names down for you…"

Chapter 9

At 1:30 that afternoon static emanated from the loud speaker in Mrs. Zebulane's classroom. Then the school secretary made an announcement:

"Attention please. Sarah McKinliy, Mariana Rodriguez, and Lizzy Zwickermin, please report to the principal's office."

Sarah cringed.

"*Somebody* is in trouble," Bonnie chirped.

Mrs. Zebulane nodded at Sarah. "You may leave."

Sarah got up. She was all too aware that every student in the room was watching her as she left the classroom and stepped out into the hallway.

The school secretary gave Sarah a nod when she arrived at the front office. Mariana and Lizzy had just arrived a few moments before she got there.

"You can go right in, girls" the school secretary said. "Principal Bruntweil is expecting you." She pointed to the door to the principal's office.

"Thanks…I guess," said Lizzy.

During their time at H.C. Stonewelle Elementary School, none of them had ever set foot in the principal's office. It was new territory. The door to the principal's office opened. The three of them hesitantly stepped into the room.

There was an institutional feel to the room with its light green walls and dark walnut wainscoting. Principal Bruntweil was seated behind a large oak desk in the center of the room. Three small folding chairs were lined up in front of the desk.

The principal looked up at the three of them. "Have a seat, girls," he said, motioning to the three chairs in front of his desk. Sarah, Mariana, and Lizzy sat down.

On top of the principal's desk were three manila folders. One for each of them. Beside the folders was the school district's *Students' Rights and Responsibilities Handbook.* And next to that was a copy of the survey.

The principal opened each folder. He perused the contents of each folder. And a few minutes later he said, "I believe this is the first visit to my office for each of you." Then he picked up the survey and looked it over…"Who is responsible for this?"

Sarah glanced at Lizzy and Mariana. Then she said, "Um...I guess I am, sir."

"Me too," Mariana admitted.

Not to be left out, Lizzy said, "I'm in on it too."

"Well girls, it's good see that all three of you are in agreement on this. That is not always the case. It makes my job easier. Now...did any of you have *permission* to distribute the survey in the cafeteria?"

Nobody answered.

"I'll take your silence as a *no*. The three of you have gone against the rules. You have broken a school rule, in fact."

Sarah gulped.

Mariana hiccupped.

Lizzy sneezed.

The principal picked up the *Students' Rights and Responsibilities Handbook*. He flipped to page five. Then he said, "The three of you have violated Rule #5. You have distributed unauthorized material on school property."

Sarah gulped again.

Mariana hiccupped once more.

Lizzy sneezed even louder.

"Now, that said, this is a relatively minor infraction. And where you girls have had no prior disciplinary issues, I'm going to write this off. This time. Let this be a lesson, girls. The next time you decide to distribute something on school property, be sure you receive permission. Come see me first."

"Yes sir."

The principal looked at the three of them. "Okay, now that the formalities are out of the way...I will tell you that your timing on this survey was good."

Sarah, Mariana and Lizzy looked at each other. *Huh?*

"You see, the school district just hired a *food services director*," the principal continued. "She will be overseeing the food services at each school in the district. The food services director starts work next week. I'm sure your survey will be of interest to her. If you care to tally the results of your survey and get them to me, I will plan to give them to the new food services director."

"You got it, sir," said Lizzy. Sarah and Mariana nodded in agreement.

"Very well, girls. You are dismissed."

On the way back to their classrooms, Sarah said, "We could tally the survey results at my house after school."

46

"Sounds like a plan," Lizzy agreed.

"Count me in," said Mariana.

"Okay, let's meet after last bell."

"Later."

*****

When they tallied the survey answers that afternoon at Sarah's house, the results were not at all surprising. The students were tired of the school lunches. They wanted a change of menu.

*****

Principal Bruntweil was in a meeting when Sarah, Mariana, and Lizzy arrived at the front office the following morning. They left the survey results with the school secretary.

"I'll be sure the principal receives them," she said. Then she whispered, "You know, the teachers and I don't care much for the cafeteria food either. I think the survey was a good idea."

"Thanks, ma'am.

Chapter 10

Sarah was at the kitchen sink washing dishes on Friday night when her mother got home from a PTO meeting. That her mother had attended a PTO meeting was not surprising. Mrs. McKinliy had always been active in her daughter's schooling. At Sarah's old school, her mother had been a *room parent* before she began teaching. And she had chaperoned field trips, participated in bake sales, and helped out with school plays and other events. Mrs. McKinliy also had been an active member of the PTO at Sarah's old school.

"Hi, sweetheart."

"Hey, Mom." Sarah was rinsing a plate under the faucet.

"I have news."

"News?"

"I have a job."

"A job?"

"Yes…I'm going to be working at your school."

Sarah dropped the plate. "What?"

"I'm going to be a *lunch lady* at your school cafeteria."

48

Oh no!

"Maybe I can help improve that food you've been complaining about," her mother said.

Sarah couldn't believe it! She immediately pictured the attention this would draw. And the teasing that would surely result when her classmates found out that she was the lunch lady's daughter. Sarah absolutely dreaded the thought of it.

"Why?!" Sarah asked. "Why do you have to be a *lunch lady?*"

Her mother smiled. "One of the lunch ladies just retired. The school had a job opening. And I need a job."

"How *long* are you going to be a lunch lady for?"

"Mrs. McKinliy shrugged. "For as long as they need me...or until I find a teaching position."

Ugh.

Mrs. McKinliy gathered her hair back in a ponytail. "I suppose I'll need to get a hair net."

You've got to be kidding. "When do you start?"

"Monday."

I can hardly wait.

Sarah was buttering a piece of toast on Saturday morning when her mother walked into the kitchen.

"Morning, sweetheart. I'm going to the salon today for a manicure. How about joining me? You could get one too. We could have lunch afterward. I heard there's a new Mexican restaurant downtown."

Sarah frowned. "Uh, no thanks. I've got some things to do," she lied.

A flash of disappointment crossed her mother's face. "Well, perhaps next weekend."

Whatever.

Sarah felt a pang of guilt, but it soon passed. She was too mad at her mother to feel guilty. Her mother wasn't exactly her favorite person right now. Of all the elementary schools in the state of Massachusetts, why did her mother have to choose to work at H.C. Stonewelle Elementary School? It was just so unfair.

*****

It had been a lousy weekend. The worst ever. All weekend long, Sarah worried about Monday—her mother's first day of work at H.C. Stonewelle Elementary School. She dreaded the thought of going to the school cafeteria on Monday. She cringed just thinking about the attention that

she'd receive when her classmates found out that her
mother was one of the lunch ladies. Attention was the last
thing in the world that Sarah wanted.

On Sunday evening, as Sarah lay awake in bed, she
watched the clock on her nightstand. Monday morning was
looming closer with each passing minute. Sarah didn't want
the weekend to end. She wanted Sunday to last forever.

With her mind so worked up, she was unable to fall
asleep. But later that evening, just before midnight...and an
idea came to her. A simple, wonderful idea. She wouldn't
go to school on Monday.

*****

When she woke up Monday morning, Sarah placed an
extra blanket on her bed. Then she practiced a few fake
coughs. After that she got back in bed and waited.

"Sarah, breakfast is ready," her mother called out.

Sarah didn't respond. She remained in bed. Her mother
called her a few minutes later, but once again Sarah did not
reply. Then her mother walked up the stairs and knocked on
the door to her room. When there was still no response, her
mother opened the door and stepped into the room.

51

"Time to get ready for school," her mother announced.

Sarah fake-coughed. "I don't feel so good."

A concerned look crossed her mother's face. She sat down on the edge of the bed and placed the back of her left hand against Sarah's forehead.

"Hmmm. You don't seem to have a fever."

"I sure feel like I do," Sarah complained.

"Open your mouth. Let me take a look at your throat."

Sarah opened her mouth. Her mom glanced at her throat. "You're fine. Time to get ready for school."

Sarah groaned.

Chapter 11

Sarah jumped when the lunch bell sounded on Monday afternoon. She was in no hurry to go to the cafeteria. She stayed in her seat as the other students rushed out of the classroom. And it wasn't lost on her teacher. "Are you okay, Sarah?" Ms. Zebulane asked. The woman was clad in bell bottom jeans and a vintage flowered shirt. Sarah suspected the woman's entire wardrobe was from the 1960s.

"Y-yes," Sarah stammered.

"You look a little pale."

"I'm okay."

"Good. You should go to the cafeteria. You don't want to miss lunch period.

I wish there was no lunch period.

Sarah's hands were clammy when she stepped into the lunch line. Her mom was ladling American chop suey onto plates. The name tag on her shirt read: Mrs. McKinliy. Sarah winced when she saw it. Surely her classmates would make the connection.

Randall Kepleire was in front of Sarah in the lunch line once again. And when he reached the serving area and saw Mrs. McKinliy, he suddenly stopped. Mrs. McKinliy was much younger than the other lunch ladies. And she was beautiful. For a second there, it seemed as if Randall might be at a loss for words. But then he said, "I'll have the grilled salmon today."

Mrs. McKinliy handed him a plate of American chop suey. "Sorry, no fish on the menu today. Here you go."

"Can't wait to dig in," Randall said, as he pushed his tray down the rail toward the register.

Mrs. McKinliy's face creased in a smile when she saw Sarah. "Hi, sweetheart!"

Sarah's face reddened in embarrassment. She wished she were anywhere else. "Hi," she whispered.

"Now I see what you mean about the food," her mom whispered as she handed Sarah a plate of American chop suey. "See you when you get home, sweetheart."

Whatever.

Sarah made a mental note to bring her lunch from home from now on. Then she quickly pushed her tray down the rail toward the cashier. She grabbed a lukewarm milk and paid the cashier. Then she nervously stepped into the lunchroom.

Sarah expected the worse. Surely, her classmates had made the connection and now knew that she was the lunch lady's daughter. She braced herself for the taunts...but surprisingly, everything seemed business as usual. There were no stares from her classmates. Nobody said anything. It seemed that nobody had picked up on the fact that she was the new lunch lady's daughter...Nobody but Randall Kepleire that is. Randall was seated at a nearby table with his friends. His face creased in a grin when he saw Sarah...He stood up.

Randall was holding a handmade megaphone—a piece of construction paper rolled up into a cone. He raised it to his mouth.

"Attention Please! Attention!"

Sarah stopped and looked over at Randall. Randall pointed at her and yelled:

"Make way for the lunch lady's daughter! The one and only...Sarah McKinliy!"

Sarah froze. She had never been so embarrassed. This was even worse than the skating incident. Laughter erupted over at Bonny's table. Then it spread through the lunchroom. Soon, practically every kid in the cafeteria was laughing at her. But not Mariana and Lizzy. They watched as Sarah emptied the contents on her lunch tray into the rubbish barrel and left the cafeteria. Sarah's eyes were watery. It was all she could do not to burst into tears.

Chapter 12

Sarah was removing her jacket from her locker just after the dismissal bell. The locker door was open; it obstructed her view down the hall. When she shut the locker door, she saw Lizzy and Mariana heading up the hall toward her. They approached her.

"You guys want to hang out this afternoon?" Lizzy asked.

"Yes," Mariana said.

Sarah shrugged. She didn't feel much like talking. The embarrassment she had felt earlier that afternoon had subsided. Now she was angry. She was angry with Randall Kepliere for embarrassing her in the cafeteria. And she was angry with Bonnie, who had started the laughter that spread like wildfire through the cafeteria. But most of all, she was angry with her mother. If her mother hadn't decided to be a lunch lady, Sarah's day would have been completely different. Of all the schools in the state of Massachusetts, why did her mother have to work at H.C. Stonewelle Elementary School? It was so unfair.

"I can't believe that stunt that Randall Kepliere pulled in the cafeteria today," Lizzy said. "That was so immature."

"Yes, it was," Mariana agreed.

"We should get him back," Lizzy said.

"How?" Mariana asked.

"I'll tell you how," Lizzy said. "We embarrass him just like he embarrassed Sarah today. A lot of kids probably don't remember, but back in third grade…Randall peed in his pants. Tomorrow at lunch I'll yell, "Hey, Randall! Do you remember that time in third grade when you peed in your pants?! That will fix him."

Sarah shook her head. "No."

"Please?" Lizzy prodded.

"No. You don't need to fight my battles. That's good to know about Randall peeing his pants, though. If he ever pulls another stunt like that, I'll be prepared with a good comeback."

Lizzy frowned. "Okay."

The three of them left school together and headed up Main Street. They stopped by the dime store. Then they headed over to Sarah's house.

When they arrived, Mrs. McKinliy was in the kitchen. She had just removed a tray of cookies from the oven. She placed the tray on the counter beside two other trays of cookies. There were three flavors of cookies on the trays: chocolate chip, peanut butter, and oatmeal.

"Good afternoon, girls," Mrs. McKinliy said, as Sarah, Mariana, and Lizzy stepped into the kitchen. "You're just in time."

"Just in time for what?" Lizzy asked.

"Just in time to sample cookies. I think that jello isn't cutting it as a desert in the school cafeteria. Cookies might be a nice change."

"Good call," said Lizzy.

Sarah didn't want to talk about school. She didn't want to think about school lunch. And she didn't want to talk to her mother.

Mrs. McKinliy removed three plates from cupboard. She handed a plate to each of the girls. "Try all three flavors if you like, girls. Tell me which one is your favorite."

"Gladly" said Lizzy. She picked a cookie from each tray. Mariana did the same.

Sarah just frowned. "I'm not hungry."

A few minutes later, Lizzy said, "Oatmeal is my choice."

"Peanut butter is my favorite," Mariana put in.

Mrs. McKinliy smiled. "And I happen to know that chocolate chip is Sarah's favorite flavor."

Sarah frowned.

"Well, you girls were not much help," Mrs. McKinliy joked. "I was hoping to narrow the choices down. At work I just have enough time to make one batch of cookies for the school lunch. Perhaps you girls could bring the cookies to school tomorrow and ask your classmates which flavor they like best. See if there is a general preference."

"You got it, Mrs. M," Lizzy said.

"This will be fun," Marianna put in.

"Whatever," Sarah said. "Let's go up to my room."

"Have fun, girls."

An hour and a half later, as they were leaving, Mrs. McKinliy handed Lizzy a tin of oatmeal cookies. Then she handed Mariana a tin of peanut butter cookies. "These are for school tomorrow," she said.

"Thanks Mrs. M!" Lizzy said.

"Yes, thanks," said Mariana.

"My pleasure, girls. Sarah, your tin is on the counter."

Sarah didn't reply.

"Let me know how it goes tomorrow, girls."

"You bet, Mrs. M."

*****

The next morning, when she arrived at school, Sarah received stares and sideways glances from kids she didn't even know. She was in the limelight now—because of Randall Kepliere. Thanks to Randall Kepliere, the entire fifth grade class now knew that Sarah was the lunch lady's daughter.

Sarah stared downward, avoiding eye contact as she made her way to her locker to stash her cookie tin. When she arrived in Room 210, Bonnie caught her eye. When Sarah sat down, Bonnie leaned over and said, "I hope for your sake that your mother makes better food at home than she does in the cafeteria."

Laughter erupted in the classroom. Sarah's face reddened in embarrassment once again.

"Quiet down," Mrs. Zebulane said, before Sarah had a chance to respond.

Sarah heard little of what Mrs. Zebulane taught that morning. Her mind was preoccupied.

When the lunch bell rang that afternoon, Sarah headed to her locker to get the cookie tin. She brought the tin to the cafeteria. When she reached the cafeteria she looked downward to avoid eye contact. Mariana and Lizzy were already sitting at the lunch table when Sarah arrived. She set her tin down on the table. Then the three of them removed the covers from the tins.

Lizzy picked up an oatmeal cookie from her tin and took a bite. "Delicious!" she shouted.

Mariana selected a peanut butter cookie from her tin. She took a bite and said, "*Muy buena*—Very good!"

Sarah's mind was still preoccupied, but she went along with the ploy. She too picked up a cookie from her tin and took a bite. "Mmmm."

The stage was set. Kids from nearby tables looked over at the three of them—and the cookie tins. Zack Trevise was sitting at the table just beyond theirs. The cookies caught his attention. He got up and walked over to the girls' table. "Can I have a cookie?" he asked.

"Sure, help yourself," said Lizzy. "Try them all. Tell your friends they can have some too…There's just one stipulation."

Zack's eyebrows lifted. "What's that?"

Lizzy flashed a smile. "You have to tell us which flavor is your favorite."

"Gladly."

Zack called to the other kids at his table. "Free cookies!"

His friends got up and headed over. "All we ask is to let us know which flavor is your favorite," Lizzy announced.

"Chocolate chip," Zack reported.

"Oatmeal," said the kid standing beside him.

"Peanut butter," another kid said.

Sarah, Mariana and Lizzy looked at each another. They were back to square one. But a few moments later, when kids at other tables saw Zack and his friends milling around the table, they became curious. Then Zack shouted, "Free cookies!" again, even louder. That's all it took. Kids from the other nearby tables got up and headed over. And then kids from other tables caught on and headed over too.

Soon, practically every kid in the cafeteria was milling around the girls' table. But Bonnie, Claire, and Lauren were not among them.

"Big deal," said Bonnie. "So they're handing out cookies. They probably came up with the idea to make friends. Good luck to them. When the cookies are gone, they'll be outcasts once again."

Claire and Lauren weren't so sure. In fact, it seemed they were missing out.

Claire stood up. "I'm going over there. Those cookies look *good*."

"I'm going too," Lauren said.

Bonnie frowned. "Not me."

"There's plenty to go around," Lizzy announced as the crowd around the table grew. "All we ask is that you tell us which flavor is your favorite." Sarah, Mariana, and Lizzy wrote a check mark on a napkin each time someone announced their favorite flavor.

Claire and Lauren made their way across the cafeteria to the table where the cookies were being distributed. They sat down across from Sarah. Sarah handed each of them a cookie tin. "Here you go."

"Thanks, Sarah."

Sarah nodded. "Enjoy."

Mr. Portrie, the art teacher, had lunch duty. He had just purchased his lunch and stepped into the lunchroom. The place was loud. Louder than usual. Almost every student in the room was gathered around a table at the opposite end of the cafeteria. He needed to put a stop to the noise. Things were getting out of hand and it was his responsibility to maintain order. The art teacher walked across the room toward the crowd. The man had almost reached the crowd when he stepped into a pool of spilled milk…and slipped. His feet went out from under him and the next thing he knew he was sitting on the floor in a pool of milk—and his lunch tray and all its contents landed on him. The man's shirt and tie were caked in mashed potatoes and gravy.

The art teacher headed to the restroom to clean up. When he returned, the cookie tins were empty. Most of the students had returned to their tables and things had quieted down.

When Sarah, Mariana, and Lizzy added up the check marks it was clear that chocolate chip was the preferred flavor.

"Okay," Lizzy said. "Let's go tell Mrs. M."

"Yes," Mariana responded.

"…All right," Sarah reluctantly agreed.

There were just two minutes left in the lunch period when Sarah, Mariana, and Lizzy stepped into the cafeteria's food service area. Mrs. McKinliy was speaking with a repairman who was fixing the milk cooler. She looked over at the girls. "Be right there. Just finishing up."

"Sure thing, Mrs. M."

Sarah glanced around. She hadn't been in the food service area for a while. She had been bringing her lunch since the day that Randall Kepliere embarrassed her in front of the entire fifth grade class.

Looking around, Sarah noted some improvements. The food serving station behind the counter seemed cleaner. The pots and pans on the shelves along the far wall were neatly organized. And the lunch trays, plates and silverware seemed cleaner than before. And it seemed there would be cold milk going forward too. But the main course—meatloaf—still looked dismal.

"Hi girls," Mrs. McKinley said, as the repairman departed. "What a nice surprise."

"Thanks, Mrs. M," said Lizzy.

"We have the results," Mariana announced.

"Results?"

"The cookie results," Lizzy clarified. "We found out what most popular flavor is."

"Great, what was it?"

"Chocolate chip."

"Okay, good to know. There's not much I can do about the main course unfortunately, but I do have a say about dessert—and it's time for a change. Thanks, girls. Oh, Sarah, I'll be home a little later than usual today. I need to be here when the milk delivery truck arrives later this afternoon."

Whatever.

Chapter 13

The following afternoon, when the fourth and fifth-graders arrived at the cafeteria for lunch, the aroma of chocolate chip cookies wafted out from the kitchen. Mrs. McKinliy had arrived at work two hours early that morning to make cookies.

And that day, for the first time that year, the kids who brought their lunch from home were envious of the kids who bought their lunch. The cookies were a welcome change from green jello with stale whipped cream.

Sarah, Mariana, Lizzy, Claire, and Lauren ate lunch together. And the five of them left school together that day too. They went to Sarah's house. This time, Mrs. McKinliy was in the kitchen spooning pudding into small bowls. "Hi girls. You're just in time."

"Just in time for what?" Claire inquired.

"Pudding sampling."

"Huh?"

Mrs. McKinliy gestured to the kitchen table. Resting on the table were assorted bowls of pudding: chocolate, vanilla and butterscotch. "I used a sugar free recipe," she said. "Try them all if you like. Let me know which flavor you prefer. I'll be back shortly."

"Gladly," Lizzy said.

"Yes, gladly," Mariana agreed.

"Count me in," said Claire.

"Me too," Lauren said.

Sarah rolled her eyes.

Mrs. McKinliy stepped back into the kitchen five minutes later. "What's the verdict, girls?"

"It's unanimous, Mrs. M," Lizzy reported.

"That's right," Mariana confirmed.

"Well?"

"Chocolate."

'Well, I'm glad you're all in agreement. It would be challenging to bring samples of pudding to school. Chocolate it will be."

The next afternoon, when the fourth and fifth-graders arrived at the cafeteria for lunch, the aroma of warm chocolate pudding wafted out from the serving area. Once again, the students who brought their lunch from home were envious of the students who bought their lunch. And interestingly, the lunch line was a little longer than the day before.

In the days that followed, as new desserts appeared on the dessert shelf, the lunch line continued to grow. And Mrs. McKinliy was becoming quite popular with the students. Thanks to Lizzy, Mrs. McKinley now had a nickname. The students were starting to call her "Mrs. M."

Sarah was coming around. She wasn't quite as self-conscious about her mother working at the school. In fact, she had to admit…her mother was doing a good job. It seemed the other students thought so too.

The following week, on Tuesday morning, just before recess, static emanated from the loud speaker in each classroom. Then the school secretary bellowed:

"Attention please. Sarah McKinliy, Mariana Rodriguez, and Lizzy Zwickermin, please report to the principal's office."

Sarah cringed. *What now?*

"*Somebody* is in trouble again," Bonnie chirped.

Mrs. Zebulane gave Sarah a friendly nod. "Go."

Sarah got up. And once again, every student in the room watched her as she left. She caught up with Mariana and Lizzy in the hallway.

On the way down the hall to the principal's office, Mariana asked, "Do you think we're in trouble because of the cookies we brought to the cafeteria?"

Lizzy shrugged. "I don't know. Principal Bruntweil said we couldn't distribute unauthorized *materials*. He didn't say anything about not being able to distribute *food*."

"Well, I guess we'll find out soon," Sarah said as they reached the front office.

The school secretary was just finishing up a phone call at the front desk. "You can go right in, girls," she said, motioning to the principal's office. "They are waiting for you."

They?

When Sarah stepped into the principal's office, she was surprised to see her mother there. Mrs. McKinliy was sitting on a chair in front of the principal's desk—the same chair that Sarah had sat on during her previous visit to the principal's office.

At first, Sarah wondered if her mother had done something wrong. But the woman didn't seem distraught. In fact, she looked happy; it seemed she was glad to be there. And Principal Bruntweil seemed to be in a good mood as well.

71

There was another woman in the room too. The woman was sitting next to Mrs. McKinliy.

Principal Bruntweil stood up as Sarah, Mariana, and Lizzy entered his office. "Good morning, girls. You know Mrs. McKinliy of course," he said, gesturing to Sarah's mother. "And this is Mrs. Cauldreye," he announced, pointing to the other woman. "Mrs. Cauldreye is our new *food services director*."

Mrs. Cauldreye got up from her chair and faced the girls. "It's good to meet you," she said. "Principal Bruntweil has shared the results of the survey you girls conducted. And I must say, the survey will be quite helpful as I get up to speed and evaluate the school lunch menu. Quite helpful indeed. I applaud your efforts, girls. I wanted to thank you personally. I also want to mention that you'll likely see a change of menu in the weeks ahead."

The woman shifted her focus to Sarah's mother. "And thank you for your efforts, Mrs. McKinliy. I understand you have made some positive changes in the short time you have worked at the school cafeteria."

Mrs. McKinliy blushed. "It was nothing. I'm glad to be of help."

Principal Bruntweil cleared his throat. "Okay, girls. A job well done. Thank you. The three of you can return to your classrooms now."

Chapter 14

On the third Monday in October, Randall Kepliere was the first student to arrive at the cafeteria for lunch. When he reached the serving area, he said, "Hi, Mrs. M."

"Hello, Randall."

Mrs. McKinley handed him a lunch plate. On the plate was a thick slice of cheese pizza, a garden salad, and a freshly-baked roll."

"Thanks, Mrs. M! This is the best lunch, yet."

"Enjoy, Randall."

"I plan to!"

Sarah was behind Randall in the lunch line. She was back to buying her lunch again. And she had become accustomed to waiting in line for her lunch. The lunch line was now much longer than it had been at the start of school.

Sarah had overheard the conversation between Randall and her mother. And she had to admit…her mom was cool. It seemed all the students thought so. They all called her "Mrs. M" now.

Her mother's face creased in a smile when she saw Sarah. "Hiya, kiddo," she said, as she handed Sarah a lunch plate.

"Hey, Mom. Thanks."

"See you when you get home, sweetheart."

"You bet. Bye, Mom."

It was no longer just Sarah, Mariana, Lizzy, Claire, and Lauren at the lunch table. Zack and his friends sat at the table now too. Their lunch table had gone from least popular to very popular in a short period of time. Practically every seat at the table was occupied. And Sarah, Mariana, and Lizzy were suddenly popular among their classmates— well, most of them anyhow.

Sarah had just arrived at the lunch table that day when Randall Kepliere stopped by. He said hi to Sarah.

"Hi, Randall."

Randall stood there for a moment as if he were at a loss for words. Then he said, "I just wanted to say…you're mom is cool."

Sarah's eyebrows lifted. "Thanks Randall. I think so too."

Randall stared at the floor. "…I'm sorry about embarrassing you that day."

75

Sarah smiled. "Apology accepted."

"See ya."

"Bye, Randall."

A few minutes after Randall left, a girl across the cafeteria headed toward the table. Sarah watched the girl as she neared the table. The girl was tall and had deep brown eyes and long blond hair.

When the girl arrived at the table, there was one seat available across from Sarah. "Can I sit here?" the girl asked.

Sarah couldn't believe it. She said, "Sure Bonnie."

Chapter 15

The following morning, just before 10:00, the students in Room 210 looked up at the clock. Mrs. Zebulane knew better than to attempt teaching anything in the final minutes before recess. When the recess bell rang at ten o'clock, the students sprang from their seats, grabbed their coats, and headed outside. Sarah wasn't among them though.

She went to the cafeteria to see her mother. The school store was having a sale that day. Sarah didn't have any money.

There were certain advantages when your mother worked at your school, Sarah was starting to realize. She had come a long way since the day her mother started working in the school cafeteria.

Her mother was pulling a tray of cookies from the oven when Sarah reached the cafeteria's kitchen. "Hey, sweetheart. I thought you'd be at recess right about now."

"I'm on my way," Sarah replied. "I just wanted to ask if I might be able to borrow some money. The school store is having a sale."

"Sure thing." Her mother extracted two dollars from her change purse and handed the money to Sarah.

"Thanks, Mom."

Mrs. McKinliy smiled. "Sure."

Just then her mother's cell phone rang. She answered it. "Hello?...Good morning...Yes...Oh?...Sure, I can meet you there...Okay, I look forward to meeting you too...Thanks...I'll see you then."

Mrs. McKinliy smiled when the call ended.

"What's up?" Sarah asked.

"That was the principal of the middle school. It seems that one of the sixth grade English teachers is retiring at the end of the second term. She asked if I had interest in interviewing for the position. What would you think of me being your English teacher next year at the middle school?"

Sarah smiled. Then she said, "That would be cool, Mom."

And she really meant it.

Made in the USA
San Bernardino, CA
23 February 2015